This picture book helps children learn about mathematical concepts through a colorful and entertaining story.

Math concepts explored may include:
• Understanding math concepts
• Time
• Explaining the passage of time during a day by the diurnal motion of sun

About the Author
Mi-ae Lee graduated from Chung Ang University in Seoul, South Korea, with a degree in creative writing. She has written many children's books and has been honored with a number of literary awards, including the Samsung Literature Award.

About the Illustrator
Yang-sook Choi graduated from Sungshin Women's University with a degree in oriental painting. In 2002, she won the grand prize in the Publishers Art Competition. She has illustrated many children's books.

Tan Tan Math Story *A Day at Grandma's*

Original Korean edition © Yeowon Media Co., Ltd

This U.S edition published in 2015 by TANTAN PUBLISHING INC,
4005 W Olympic Blvd, Los Angeles, CA 90019-3258

U.S and Canada Edition © TANTAN PUBLISHING INC in 2015

ISBN: 978-1-939248-10-7

Printed in South Korea at Choil Munhwa Printing Co., 12 Seongsuiro 20 gil, Seongdong-gu, Seoul.

A Day at Grandma's

Written by Mi-ae Lee   Illustrated by Yang-sook Choi

TanTan Publishing

It is **dawn**, and the sky is slowly getting brighter. The darkness of night is gone, and a new day has begun.

Mommy gazes from the balcony at home. "Yujin, you are at Grandma's," she says to the small birds flying by. "I wonder what your day will be like, little one."

I am thinking about my mother. "Mommy, I can smell the fresh air of **dawn**," I say. "Grandma is already awake and has gone out to the yard."

The birds chirp. The roosters crow *cock-a-doodle-doo*. And the church bells ring *ding-dong, ding-dong*.

At Grandma's house, even with my eyes closed I know it is **dawn**. The sounds signal the start of a new day. I open my eyes and glance around. But I am not ready to wake up! "Mommy, I want to go back to sleep," I whisper, as I close my eyes.

Describe specific visual details for different times of day—for example, darkness fading or the sky brightening at dawn. By doing so you can help children understand the concept of time change.

Although she is far away, my mother is thinking about me.

"Sweetie, it is **morning**," she says. "It's the time when the mist clears and golden sun rays pour down on every tree leaf. The birds are awake, and they are singing. It is the time of day when you rub your sleepy eyes and run to me. I already miss you, dear Yujin."

It is **morning**. Although she is far away, I am thinking about my mother.

I hear the *clank-clank-clank* of a fork as Grandma stirs eggs in a bowl. I smell the delicious scent of Grandma's pot of stew sizzling on the stove.

Grandpa gently strokes my forehead, and I open my eyes. My mother is usually the first person I see when I wake up. But Mommy is back at home. I scurry to the kitchen and tightly hug Grandma. "I love you, Grandma," I say. But I miss my mommy.

It is **almost noon** and the bright sun shines down on roofs, mountains, and forests from high in the sky. My mother is still thinking of me. She knows that when the sun shines in my eyes, I squint and make shade with my hand.

"I wonder what you are doing now, sweet Yujin," Mommy says.

When different times of day are described in the story, encourage the children to talk about what they do during those times: morning, noon, afternoon, and evening. By having them remember and say various activities, they will begin to understand the concept of time.

It is **noon** now. The sun is at its peak making my shadow hide under my feet. Uncle and I are trying to catch fish in the brook. The sun feels warm on the top of my head. My legs and feet feel cool in the water. It is fun to splash—even though the noise scares the fish.

Ah, I hear my stomach growling—I am hungry! My grandmother calls me for lunch, just like Mommy does. "Time to eat, dear Yujin!" she says.

It is now **afternoon**. Usually after we eat a delicious lunch, the sun begins to lower slowly in the sky. Mommy knows it's time for me to snuggle in bed for a peaceful nap. I wonder if Mommy is thinking about me now. Of course she is!

"Yujin, the house feels empty and time goes by so slowly without you," Mommy says.

It is still **afternoon**. But My shadow has grown longer. Even though it's time for my nap, I am not sleepy—I'm catching dragonflies! A dragonfly flutters its wings on my fingertip. I see many other bugs in the grass.

"Watch me, Grandma," I say as I run after another dragonfly.

The day has passed quickly, and now it is
dusk. A cooler breeze blows in the park.
The sun is sinking behind the mountain. The
sunset glows red in the western sky.

"Yujin," Mommy says to the breeze, "even
though you have been gone just one day, I
miss you so much. Hurry home to me!"

It is **evening**. I see the lights turn on, one by one, along the dim street. It has gotten dark quickly. Daddy is driving. He says we still have a long way to go before we will be home. *Honk! Honk!* The cars are moving so slowly. We are stuck in the traffic. I miss Mommy.

The **night** has come. The moon is shining gently in the night sky.

"Yujin, I am waiting for you," Mommy says quietly. She sits on a wooden bench and watches for Daddy and me. "Every time I hear a car, I hope it means you are home at last."

And then, at last, I *am* home!
"Mommy!" I say, and I run to her.

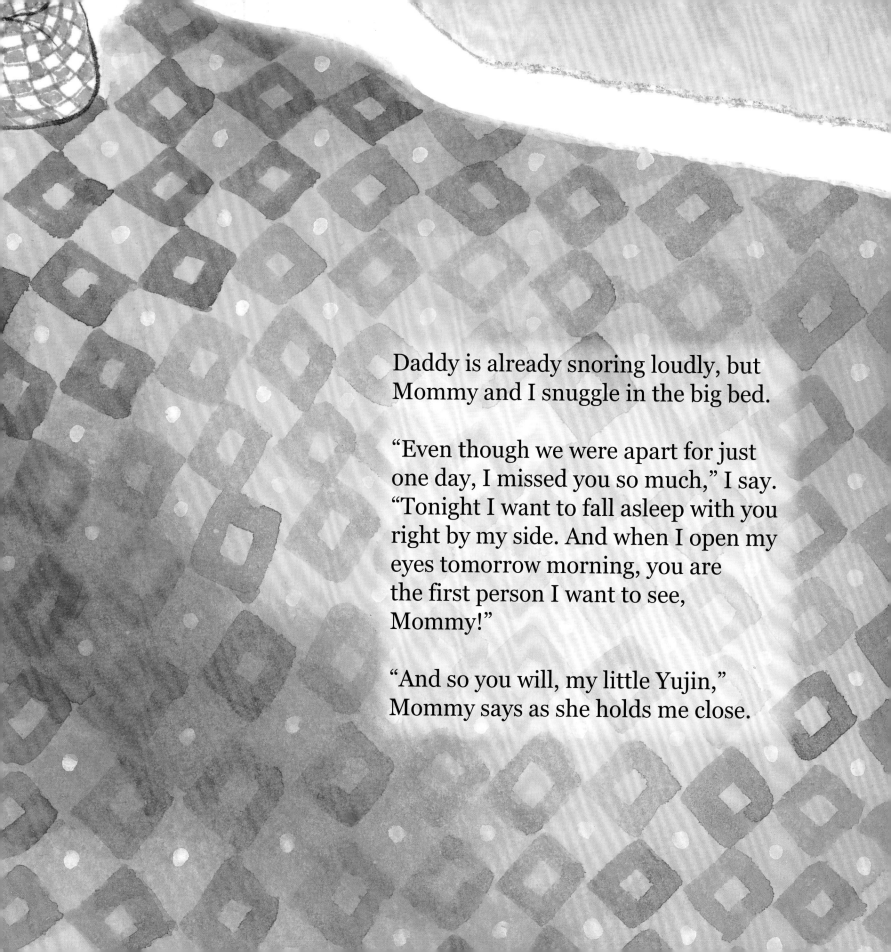

Daddy is already snoring loudly, but Mommy and I snuggle in the big bed.

"Even though we were apart for just one day, I missed you so much," I say. "Tonight I want to fall asleep with you right by my side. And when I open my eyes tomorrow morning, you are the first person I want to see, Mommy!"

"And so you will, my little Yujin," Mommy says as she holds me close.

Concept of Time—One Day

At the age when children begin to understand the order of events, they also start to understand day and night and the cycle of the seasons. Children do not typically think of a day in terms of minutes or other units of time. They instead form a concept of time based on their daily routines and activities, such as waking up, eating, going to preschool, playing, and reading.

To understand the temporal relationship of each event, children should be encouraged to use various vocabulary words that are associated with the continuity of time. Use terms such as *before* and *after; yesterday, today,* and *tomorrow; first, now,* and *later.* When your child wakes up in the morning, talk about what he/she might do based on the time of day: for example, "What is the first thing you need to do when you wake up in the morning?" or "What will you do before you eat lunch?" With such prompting, children will begin to think about what they do and how they spend their day as they experience changes in their surroundings. Before your child goes to bed, have him/her reflect on how he/she spent the day. By repeating this process over time, your child will become more familiar with the concept of a day and its inherent changes.

Morning, Afternoon, and Evening Hopscotch Game

| **Activity Goal** | To learn about aspects of time that relate to daily routines
| **Materials** | 2 hopscotch pebbles, chalk

	Sky	
7 Out!		8 Night
	6 Evening	
4 Afternoon		5 Out!
	3 Morning	
1 Dawn		2 Out!
	Ground	

1 Draw this figure on a flat space on the ground and write in the times of day, from dawn to night, in the spaces as detailed.

2 After choosing who goes first, the first player starts by carrying a pebble and hopping on one leg, starting from Ground and then hopping in all the spaces until he/she reaches Sky. When the player reaches Sky, he/she stands with both feet on the ground, and without looking behind him/her, throws the hopscotch pebble in the direction of the spaces.

3 If the pebble lands on Out!, the next player takes a turn. If the pebble lands on any space other than Out!, the player turns around, returns to the Ground area, and states an activity/routine related to the space the pebble landed on. The player must describe a routine or action that is associated with the designated time of day.

4 Once the player describes an appropriate daily routine that links to the designated time of day, he/she may pick up the pebble and indicate his/her Break Spot by marking it with an X or O. The Break Spot is where the player may "rest" by putting both feet down. After indicating the Break Spot, the player returns to the Ground area with his/her pebble.

5 Continue playing in the same way. The player who describes the daily routine most accurately (and thereby acquires the most Break Spots) is the winner.

 My Day

As the lightly floating sun goes down behind the mountain, the moon rises. My day flows, too, following the rhythm of the sun and moon. Notice the changes in each day.

Dawn is the time when the dark sky outside the window slowly brightens.

Morning is the time when the mist clears away and golden sun rays pour down on every tree leaf.

Noon is the time when the bright sun shines down upon the roofs and mountains and forests from high in the sky.

Afternoon is the time when the hot sun that was at its peak begins to lower slowly in the sky.

Dusk is the time when a cool breeze blows and the sun sinks behind the mountain.

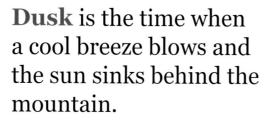

Night is the time when the moon gently shines down on the dark world.

What Did I Do Then?

Yesterday, Mommy and I played together making sand castles. What did I do after that?

I washed my hands.

I played in the sand.

When it was almost time for bed tonight, I brushed my teeth. What did I do before that?

I ate dinner.

I read a story with Mommy.

I do many different things during the day. In the picture below, what do I usually do during the time marked with a big question mark?

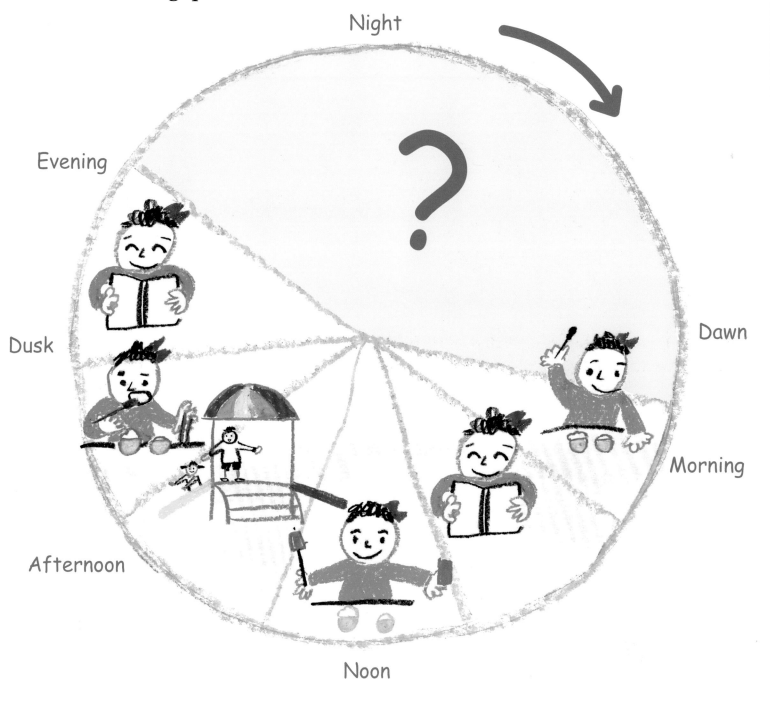